The Killick

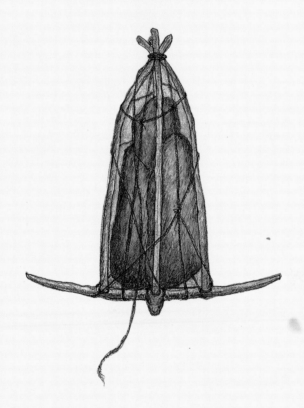

**To my parents
and all grandparents everywhere**

Published in Canada by Tundra Books, *McClelland & Stewart Young Readers*,
481 University Avenue, Toronto, Ontario M5G 2E9

Published in the United States by Tundra Books of Northern New York,
P.O. Box 1030, Plattsburgh, New York 12901

Library of Congress Catalog Number: 95-60982

Canadian Cataloguing in Publication Data

Butler, Geoff, 1945 –
    The killick : a Newfoundland story

ISBN 0-88776-449-5

I. Title.

PS8553.U699K5   1998   jC813'54   C97-932784-9
PZ7.B8Ki   1998

We acknowledge the support of the Canada Council for the Arts for our publishing program.

Printed in Hong Kong by South China Printing Co. Ltd.

1 2 3 4 5 6   03 02 01 00 99 98

The Killick
a Newfoundland story

Geoff Butler

Tundra Books

Chapter I

In Newfoundland a bedlamer is a young seal. It can also mean a young boy. In the small community where George lives he is proud to be called a bedlamer, for he is as much at home on the water as a seal is.

Whenever spring showed its nose around the corner, George was eager to help launch his grandfather's dory. This year was special because now that he was twelve, his grandfather had handed the whole job over to him, saying, "I know when to give way to a better man."

By the time most of the snow had melted and the warm sun was out nearly every day, George had already spruced up the dory from its winter layup and orchestrated the help of neighbors to move it into the water.

"With such grand weather, I can see why you want to get it out early," his grandfather said. "I'm as stiff as a board myself after being cooped up all winter."

Nearly everyone called the old man Skipper Fred. Even George's father, when he phoned from Toronto where he went to find work after the cod fishery closed, always asked: "And how's the Skipper?" The only exceptions were George's mother, who called him "Dad," and George who called him "Grandpa."

Skipper Fred often looked longingly at the distant island across the bay where he'd lived most of his life. So George was not surprised one spring morning when his grandfather said: "George, my boy, could you take me over to the island this fine day? I'd like to visit your Grandma's grave."

George's mother looked worried. "Dad, are you sure that's wise? It's still pretty early in the year, you know. I hear there's ice offshore and if the wind comes up, it could get nasty."

"We'll be back before supper time. George is as good in a boat as ever I was. Right, George? If the weather changes, we'll stay overnight on the island. There's a few families left there."

George's mother is still uneasy, but, as someone used to the sea, she says: "Don't be late then and don't go taking any unnecessary chances."

As they gather things together for the trip, George sees his grandfather slip his war medals into his pocket and wonders why. The last time he saw his grandfather take out his medals was last November 11, Armistice Day as they still call it in Newfoundland.

That morning George had stood near the window, looking out at the gulls and the weather. Their house perched on rocky cliffs facing the harbor and gusts of wind were sweeping in from the open sea, hitting the windows broadside with dull thuds and whistling through the crevices in the loose-fitting window frames.

Skipper Fred, sitting in his rocking chair, was also looking out, "Cold and damp. Another one, cold and damp," he had remarked. "Would it be asking too much, Lord, for a warm, sunny Armistice Day once in a while?" Then he added, referring to the medals on his chest, "For all the polishing I've done, not a one will sparkle in this weather."

Then the old man seemed to cheer up as he pointed down to the water where children were pulling fish lines through cracks in the stage head with jerky arm movements. "I used to do the same thing on my father's stage. When I see them, I think of coming back in for molasses on hot bread from my mother's kitchen. I can still smell it."

He might have gone on, but George's mother had interrupted. "Time to head out, Dad," she said, "if you want to be in that parade." She fastened the poppy more securely to his lapel.

"I haven't missed one yet, girl," he had replied.

George had helped his grandfather out of the chair, noticing as he always did how the old man managed with his artificial leg. At the door his grandfather braced himself against the blast of rain and wind. "I don't know why a day for remembering the sacrifices of war can't be done just as well under better weather. But maybe it's appropriate."

George knew what he meant. The war injury that cost him his leg was an inconvenience, wasn't it? So maybe Armistice Day shouldn't be too comfortable.

Once outside in the cold air, the old man had joked: "Ah, this is just what the doctor ordered." He had walked briskly, surprisingly so, as if wearing the medals and the veteran's beret gave him the strength to march like a parading soldier.

George liked his grandfather's stories of when he had gone back to fishing after the war. Another fisherman had joshed him: "Now, there, Fred, you get a patch to wear over an eye to go with that one leg of yours, and you'll cut a fine figure on the water."   And his grandfather had gone along with the pirate reference and growled: "Har, har, me matey, I could handline as good as any of you with no legs at all."

But the leg Skipper Fred had lost to a land mine in Italy in World War II was small suffering compared to what his father had gone through in the First World War. George knew his great-grandfather had done his service in muddy, rat-infested trenches in France and that he had nightmares off and on for the rest of his life, waking up thinking rats were gnawing at his feet or that he heard a wounded man crying.

George knew many other stories about his great-grandfather and World War I and, most particularly, the story of his medals. George was so shocked the evening he first heard it, he remembered exactly where he had been sitting with his grandfather down on the stage as he listened.

His great-grandfather had gone back to sealing each spring after World War I, as Newfoundlanders had been doing for more than a hundred and fifty years. When protesters trying to stop the seal hunt called Newfoundland sealers "barbarians," he went on to anyone who would hear him.

"Sure, 'twas a slaughter," Skipper Fred imitated his father's voice as he told the story, "but we was lambs to da slaughter overseas 'tween men. We was considered civilized 'nuff den, to answer da call, I'll tell ya."

Skipper Fred explained: "He couldn't understand how he was awarded medals and honors for clubbing and bayoneting people, and be called a barbarian for killing seals. He talked about the annihilation of the Newfoundland Regiment at Beaumont Hamel during the battle of the Somme: 'More like it, we was da seals.'"

Skipper Fred had paused, sitting there on the rotting wharf, before going on: "I never saw him so agitated. He finally got so mad he took his medals and used them as sinkers on a cast-net. That caused quite a stir, I can tell you. Sacrilege, it was, some people said. Then he changed that little verse about sticks and stones breaking bones but calling names never hurting, and told me, whatever I put on his tombstone, to make sure that that was there."

George was glad Skipper Fred didn't feel that way about his World War II medals as the three of them walked toward the memorial. From as far back as he could remember, George had been attending the services, for his father was always one of those who laid wreaths. When he was very small his father put him on his shoulders so he could see over the crowd. But his father was no longer around. Like so many other Newfoundland fishermen who found themselves with empty nets, he had left to work on the Canadian mainland. So George had asked if he could lay a wreath.

There had been no crowd at the memorial this past November. The ranks had been getting thinner every year as veterans died or got too feeble to come.

Skipper Fred went to join his comrades-in-arms as George and his mother took up places to the side of the memorial. The veterans, led by a color party bearing the flags and a single snare drummer, had timed their march so as to arrive at the memorial just before the eleventh hour. The rain had not stopped. No matter. George was sure he could hear his grandfather singing louder than all the others:

> O, God, our help in ages past,
> Our hope for years to come,
> Our shelter from the stormy blast,
> And our eternal home!

Once, after another rainy Armistice service, Skipper Fred had remarked: "There's nothing like singing that hymn in the pelting rain to make you feel helpless and groping, like you're on a windswept deck on a stormy sea at the mercy of God Almighty."

By the time the names of the fallen were recited and the wreaths laid, everyone had wet cheeks and runny noses, if not from weeping then from the cold rain.

Chapter II

A dory with an inboard engine is not commonly seen nowadays, but over the years Skipper Fred has kept his in fine trim, not just out of nostalgia but, as he says, "She's as good a boat as ever water wet." He allowed it was sometimes temperamental, but that was not enough reason to ditch it and upgrade to something else. With any luck the engine would be as keen to get going as they were that spring morning, and, indeed, it does respond favorably to George's familiar touch.

Once in open water, the spray bellows over the cuddy where lunch and a few emergency provisions are stored: bits of hard-tack, matches, a knife and some fishing line and hooks, along with the killick. Skipper Fred often talked of the days before the war when the sea was the only link with the outport fishing villages as well as their main source of food.

Now he shouts over the sound of the motor: "Better than traveling by car, eh George?" and begins to sing:

> I's the b'y that builds the boat,
> I's the b'y that sails 'er...

Now and then, slob ice scrapes by the boat, sounding like coarse sandpaper accompaniment. Off in the distance they can see broad spans of floating white ice.

It is more like fall than spring at the cemetery. The snow is gone, swept from the hill, but it is still too cold for the grass to appear.

"Your Grandma wanted to be buried here on the island," Skipper Fred says. "'My real home,' she liked to say."

He goes directly to his wife's grave and looks at it for a few minutes.
Then George sees him take out his war medals, pin them on his jacket,
throw back his shoulders to stand straight as a soldier at attention and salute.

George leaves his grandfather to this private moment and walks around the gravestones. He searches for his great-grandfather's grave and reads the inscription:

> Sticks and stones can break my bones,
> But there's more pain in calling names.

Skipper Fred comes to join him and they stare together at the stone.
"You see how really mad he was about being called a barbarian for hunting seals?" he said.

He unpins the medals from his jacket, puts them back in his pocket and smiles in explanation: "Your grandmother was very proud of these."

They sit on the top of the hill where they have a bite to eat and look down at the village below. Skipper Fred points out the one-room schoolhouse, the hall where "the times" were held and where community suppers were followed by floor-stomping dancing to the music of a fiddler or accordion player; the merchant's store, the wharf where the fish were culled and the bartering took place, and the fishermen's stages scattered about.

Suddenly, he stops: "I think the wind's coming up a little, George. We'd best be heading back."

Chapter III

On the way back to the boat, they wave to Isaac as they pass his house.

Skipper Fred still wants to talk about his wife. "You know, we were comrades-in-arms. And we were comrades in life, too, which is even more important. Did I ever tell you, when I came to in the field hospital after they lopped off my leg, she was the first person I saw? She was holding my hand and smiling. 'I'm from Newfoundland, too,' her first words were. I'd never seen her before, thought maybe I'd gone to heaven, she was so beautiful. Did I ever tell you that, George?"

George had heard it before. His grandfather was fond of telling it, as if he relived the moment each time. Instead of answering, George says: "I was reading dates on the gravestones, Grandpa. People died young then, didn't they?"

"Yes," Skipper Fred says. "For all the good times back then, it was a hard life and little doctoring. Families were big so they'd have better odds of seeing some of their children live to grow up. We had to travel in summer by boat or in winter by horse and sleigh on the ice to get to a doctor. It was better after the war when your grandma started nursing up and down the coast. The cottage hospitals were around and health care was in better shape."

They reach the stage. George helps his grandfather into the boat. "We'll be back in time for a game of checkers before supper, George. Now, open her up, boy."

George starts the motor and points the bow homeward. As the boat picks up speed, he notices pans of ice floating about.

It is smooth going for a while, but, farther out, the seas get rougher and they get into their rain gear to protect themselves from the spray off the bow and the tops of waves that leap over the gunwales.

They are well into the bay when the trouble starts. The engine sputters and, after a few asthmatic gasps, dies out. The boat drifts as George tries to restart the motor.

The wind, shifting about, starts to bring in a few snowflakes. George keeps struggling desperately with the motor. He realizes they are in for some bad weather. He considers rowing, but Skipper Fred motions toward the sail and starts to crawl forward. He shouts out: "We'll run with the wind, George, and put ashore further down. Keep a firm hand on the tiller. With any luck, we'll stay ahead of the ice."

Skipper Fred loosens the sail as George tries to keep the rudder steady. But the wind quickly brings in more ice that slams against the dory. The snow is now so heavy, George can hardly see his grandfather trying to work the sail.

The dory is tossed violently against jagged slabs of ice. Suddenly, there is an ominous crunch as the hull is pierced. Then, just as quickly, a swirling squall catches the sail and lifts them. More ice moves in and becomes wedged under the other side of the dory.

George scrambles onto the ice and helps his grandfather get out. Together they pry up the dory with the oars, inch by inch, using the killick as the fulcrum. They stabilize the boat against the wind and get in under it, huddling together.

The wind howls and the snow swirls around them. But at last, with their heads close together, they can hear each other speak.

"Not to worry, George," Skipper Fred says, his arms around his grandson. "We seem to be on a sizable ice floe. When we don't show up for supper, there'll be a search party on its way. I don't think we'll be going anywhere like this. At least not down." He hugs George tighter. "Are you warm enough?"

"How will a search party ever find us?" George asks. "The weather and the seas will be too bad for them even to leave home."

"Be that as it may, George, they'll find us soon enough. We're safe here on the ice, so let's just concentrate on staying warm." He takes some hard-tack from his pocket, holds it out to George, and grins: "Care for some supper?"

George realizes his grandfather is trying to sound encouraging, but the wind has changed direction and he is scared. How far out to sea, how far away from land is the ice floe being pushed? Will the ice hold under them? He tries to remember being in this kind of trouble before, but he can't. It's like nothing he's ever known. He remembers his grandfather's words about singing that hymn, "O God, our help in ages past," at a memorial service. That's what it's like, he thinks to himself. Like you're on a windswept deck in a stormy sea at the mercy of God Almighty.

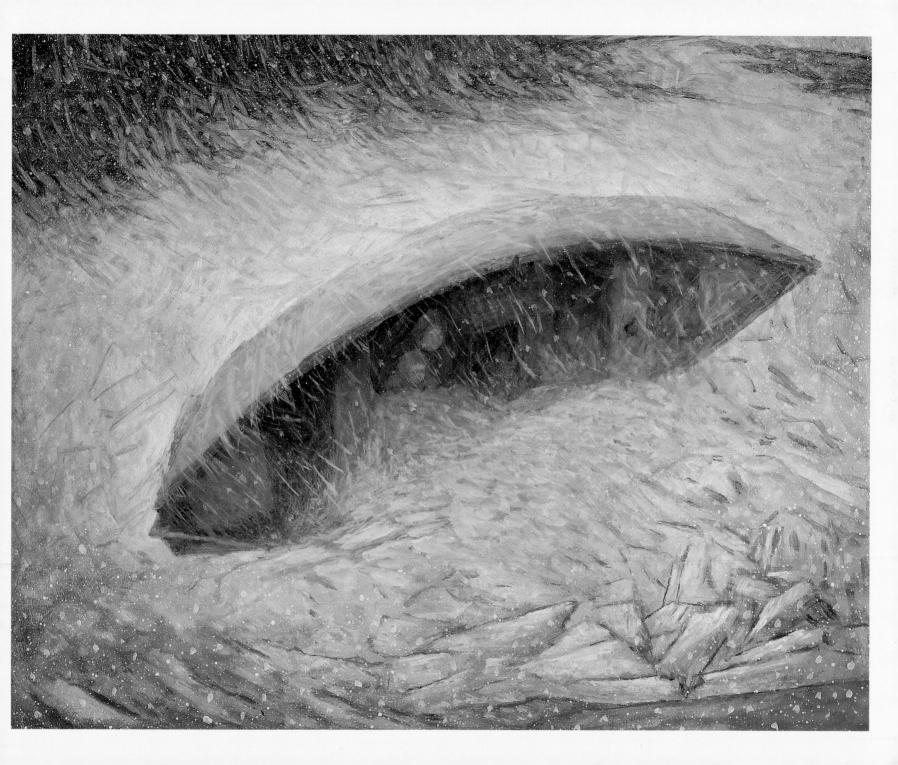

They settle in as best they can, huddling together in their windbreak. Time goes by slowly. The snow becomes so thick at times they can barely see out. Darkness sets in. Skipper Fred dozes off, but George is too scared to sleep.

He remembers an old fisherman describing how he once sat in a lifeboat, wondering if he'd be rescued. "When there's nothing you can do except wait and hope, think of something you're proud you did. We Newfoundlanders have no trouble with that, do we?" But George had never known war or danger to be brave in. What could he be proud of, he wonders. Maybe of laying that wreath after a classmate had made fun of him when he said he was going to. The words still hurt:

> Georgie, porgie, pudding and pie
> Sat on a poppy and cried and cried.
> In Flanders fields, he dropped the torch
> And now his underwear is scorched.
> Pudgy Georgie runs away
> When the real boys come out to play.

When George told his mother about it, she had said that sticks and stones break bones, but names never hurt. But his grandfather had interrupted. "Names do hurt," he had said. "My father was hurt when he was called a barbarian. And in war, it's easier to kill people by calling them names. Makes them seem not like real people."

George was proud he decided to go ahead and lay that wreath, no matter how much he was ridiculed. Maybe a wreath can commemorate the innocent victims of war on both sides.

The next day, the weather remains fierce. There'll be no one out looking for them in this. They sit in their shelter, waiting and listening for the wind to drop. How far out to sea have they been swept by now?

Suddenly, Skipper Fred holds up his hand: "I thought I heard seals barking out on the ice." He listens again: "It can't be. It's too late in the spring. They'll have gone north."

"You know," Skipper Fred continues, "my father sealed with Captain Bob Bartlett once. Now there was a master mariner and, by all accounts, a very decent man who would do anything to save his men. Mind you, he didn't have the reputation of being the greatest sealing captain, but did you know he went with Peary in his attempts to reach the North Pole? Once, when Captain Bob lost his ship trapped in ice north of Siberia, he traveled by dogsled over the ice to Alaska to get help. Too bad they didn't have helicopters and things like that to help, like we have now, eh?"

George realizes his grandfather is telling him this to sound encouraging. But he knows the other side of the story. He had read of the hundreds of men who were lost while seal hunting, of ships that had burned when seal oil caught fire or were busted up by the ice and sank, or were caught in storms on ice floes and driven out to sea — as they were being driven now.

His grandfather talks on: "I never went sealing, only fishing for the cod. But I know from my father what a hard, bloody business it was. You'd wonder why anyone, if they had their druthers, would want to go. Go? Why, they would leap at the chance to get a berth on a sealing ship but, believe me, they weren't the ones getting rich from it. They had mouths to feed at home, and there was no dole in those days to help you over rough times. No sirree. I suppose that's why my father got so upset when he heard the sealers being called barbarians."

Later, the snow lets up a little but the wind is still strong. Now and then there is the cracking sound of ice splitting up. George can feel the small pan moving under them, like a raft carrying them further out to sea.

"Hand me the oar there, George," Skipper Fred says. He pulls himself up and goes outside the shelter, using the oar to balance himself. George watches him move about the ice, poking it every so often to see how strong it is.

As another night approaches, the sound of water lapping around the edges of the ice becomes clearer. How much longer can the pan support the weight of the two of them? George asks if they should nudge the boat off if the pan gets smaller, but his grandfather shakes his head. They need it for shelter from the wind.

His grandfather wants to talk: "I've been thinking, George. When it's my time to go, I want you to use a killick for my tombstone. Put it beside my wife's stone. It's a proper marking for an old fisherman. Besides, a killick's made of sticks and stones. That wreath you laid for all the innocent victims of war, I'd like the killick to commemorate them, too, all those nameless people that were called names."

His grandfather fumbles about in his pocket for his medals. George watches as the old man rubs his cold hands together before managing awkwardly to pin the medals to his rain jacket.

They settle in for another night. George does not mention how hungry he is as he tries to sleep.

Suddenly and unexpectedly, the ice pan surges forward, jarring George awake. His grandfather is no longer beside him.

"Grandpa, Grandpa," he shouts. He moves out of the boat shelter, looks around and sees that he is alone.

As the weather gradually lets up during the morning, George sees how small the ice pan has gotten and realizes what his grandfather had done for him.

Miserably, he sits watching pans of ice floating about, rocking back and forth with the waves on the cold, gray water and, remembering the words his grandfather had used the day before, he realizes it was his grandfather's way of saying goodbye.

"The crests and troughs of the sea," he had said, "are like a rocking cradle, George, and that's what nourished the Newfoundland culture. Over the centuries, it rocked and rocked, molding the Newfoundland character, which knows as well as any that the sea which gives so much is also merciless in what it takes. And every now and then, it calls to find out what you're made of, almost as though it's trying to determine what kind of a job it did."

Toward afternoon, George hears the put-put-put of a motor in the distance. He stands up and waves his arms frantically.

Before long, he is drinking hot cocoa in the cabin of a rescue boat and is heading back home, with the killick of his grandfather's dory at his feet.

Glossary

cape-ann	fisherman's *oil-skin* hat; also called a sou'wester
cast-net	a small net thrown into the sea to catch fish, particularly caplin, a bait for cod
cuddy	a small enclosed space in the forward or aft of an undecked fishing boat
culling fish	grading dried codfish according to size and quality
dole	(to be "on the dole") public relief, or welfare
fisherman's stage	a small building, usually with a wharf, where cod was cleaned and salted
gunwales	the upper edge of the side of a boat
handline	to fish from a single line with one or two baited hooks (as opposed to net fishing)
hard-tack	a thick biscuit baked without salt and kiln-dried so that it does not go stale on long voyages
ice floe	a large, floating piece of flat ice capable of supporting people (could be part of a larger ice-field)
ice pan	a smaller flat-topped piece of floating ice (could be part of a larger *ice floe)*
in-board engine	a boat engine that is inside the vessel as opposed to the more common "out-board" engine
oil-skins	cotton that has been treated with oil and made waterproof, worn as raingear by fishermen
outport	one of the small fishing villages that dot the coast of Newfoundland and Labrador; many are now threatened by the closure of the fisheries
slob-ice	heavy, slushy mass of ice and snow that floats on the sea

Background

Newfoundland is rocky, bleak and beautiful with just over half a million people scattered along a coastline equal to that of the United States, in a Canadian province larger than Germany.

Centuries before Columbus "discovered" America, Vikings visited and briefly settled on Newfoundland's shores. Over the last two centuries fishermen from Britain and Ireland (the Irish accent can still be heard in Newfoundland speech) settled in 1300 little outports scattered around the island and up the coast of Labrador, most of them reachable only by boat. Cod was the main source of food and the main source of income, with the annual seal hunt providing a small supplement each spring.

Following World War II—in which Newfoundlanders volunteered and served out of all proportion to their population, as they had done in World War I—major changes took place. In 1949, Newfoundland joined Canada and became the tenth province.

Between 1946 and 1975, 307 outports were closed because of their isolation and the high cost of servicing them, and 28,000 residents were resettled in larger centers.

The spring seal hunt had been going on every year since the late 1700s and reached its zenith in 1857 when 13,000 men took 600,000 seals. In the 1960s it came under attack by protesters who convinced countries to boycott fur and other seal products. The hunt declined steadily and, in 1983 the last Newfoundland ship "went to the ice."

More serious was the decline of the cod fishery which had been the mainstay of Newfoundland from its beginnings. In 1992, in a last desperate effort to save the fish from extinction, the federal government was forced to close all fishing for cod, throwing thousands of fishermen and fish packers out of work. At the present time, the people are seeking to develop other industries to replace their loss.